Tadpoles
Nursery Rhymes

# Incy Wincy Spider

and

# Incy Wincy Beetle

# Notes for adults

**TADPOLES NURSERY RHYMES** are structured to provide support for newly independent readers. The books may also be used by adults for sharing with young children.

The language of nursery rhymes is often already familiar to an emergent reader, so the opportunity to see these rhymes in print gives a highly supportive early reading experience. The alternative rhymes extend this reading experience further, and encourage children to play with language and try out their own rhymes.

**If you are reading this book with a child, here are a few suggestions:**

1. Make reading fun! Choose a time to read when you and the child are relaxed and have time to share the story.

2. Recite the nursery rhyme together before you start reading. What might the alternative rhyme be about? Why might the child like it?

3. Encourage the child to reread the rhyme, and to retell it in their own words, using the illustrations to remind them what has happened.

4. Point out together the rhyming words when the whole rhymes are repeated on pages 12 and 22 (developing phonological awareness will help with decoding language) and encourage the child to make up their own alternative rhymes.

5. Give praise! Remember that small mistakes need not always be corrected.

First published in 2008 by
Franklin Watts
338 Euston Road
London NW1 3BH

Franklin Watts Australia
Level 17/207 Kent Street
Sydney NSW 2000

Text (Incy Wincy Beetle)
© Wes Magee 2008
Illustration © Tomislav Zlatic 2008

The rights of Wes Magee to be identified as the author of Incy Wincy Beetle and Tomislav Zlatic as the illustrator of this Work have been asserted in accordance with the Copyright, Designs and Patents Act, 1988.

ISBN 978 0 7496 8034 3 (hbk)
ISBN 978 0 7496 8040 4 (pbk)

**Series Editor:** Jackie Hamley
**Series Advisor:** Dr Hilary Minns
**Series Designer:** Peter Scoulding

Printed in China

Franklin Watts is a division of
Hachette Children's Books
an Hachette Livre UK company.
www.hachettelivre.co.uk

# Incy Wincy Spider

**Retold by Wes Magee**
**Illustrated by Tomislav Zlatic**

**FRANKLIN WATTS**
LONDON•SYDNEY

## Tomislav Zlatic

"Minibeasts are great!
They've got so many legs.
Some have 6, some 8 and
some many more!
I bet they buy lots
of shoes..."

# Incy Wincy spider climbing up the spout.

Down came the
raindrops,

and washed the
spider out.

7

Out came the sunshine,
and dried up all the rain.

# Now Incy Wincy spider goes up the spout again!

11

# Incy Wincy Spider

Incy Wincy spider
climbing up the spout.
Down came the raindrops,
and washed the spider out.
Out came the sunshine,
and dried up all the rain.
Now Incy Wincy spider
goes up the spout again!

Can you point to the rhyming words?

# Incy Wincy Beetle

by Wes Magee
Illustrated by Tomislav Zlatic

## Wes Magee

"Lots of beetles make homes in my garden shed where it is warm and dry, and spiders climb up the plug-hole in the bath!"

# Incy Wincy beetle playing on the wall.

Down came the
snowflakes,

and made the
beetle fall.

Here comes the wind
to blow the snow away.

19

Now Incy Wincy beetle
is climbing up to play!

20

# Incy Wincy Beetle

Incy Wincy beetle
playing on the wall.
Down came the snowflakes,
and made the beetle fall.
Here comes the wind
to blow the snow away.
Now Incy Wincy beetle
is climbing up to play!

Can you point to the
rhyming words?

# Puzzle Time!

Can you tell what these weather signs mean?

# Answers

rain

snow

sunshine
and rain

sunshine

storms